Lockdown Chronicles

Flairs and Glairs

Publication House

"Lockdown Chronicles"

ISBN No: " 978-93-91438-12-8"
1st Edition
Language – English and Hindi

Flairs and Glairs
Publication House
Regd. Under MSME Act.

Disclaimer

This is a work of fiction and solely represent the thoughts of the corresponding authors of the articles. Our editors have tried their best to edit the content of all the authors and check the plagiarism.

All the write-ups in this book are unique and are only published in this book.

In case any plagiarism   or error is found, only the author is responsible alone, and not the publisher or the Compilers.

Cover Designing and Book Formatting
Shubham Shah and Ishani Agarwal

Co Authors

Shubham Shah (Founder Flairs and Glairs)
Ishani Agarwal (Co Founder Flairs and Glairs)
Dr. Lavnya Krishnamurthy (Compiler)
Prabal Tandon (Compiler)

1. Author Urvashi Tandon
2. Author Sudiksha Choudury
3. Author Sandeep Bhadange
4. Author Sugapriya Rajesh
5. Author Namrata Naresh
6. Author Rajiv Sharma
7. Author Anjali Kavthekar
8. Author Sripremraj Sinnaiah
9. Author Anubhav Bakshi
10. Author Deepa Ravi
11. Author Narendra Goel
12. Author Pallavi Sharma
13. Author Jyothsna Krishnamurthy
14. Author Suyog Vankudre
15. Author Ruth Grace Samuel
16. Author Godwin Alex Kiruba
17. Author Bhadresh Dani
18. Author Mallikarjun Chaturvedi
19. Author Niranjan Nikhil Belamkar
20. Author Shreshta Pyaram

Shubham Shah

(Founder- Flairs and Glairs)

Shubham Shah, an entrepreneur at "Flairs & Glairs" a brand with dynamics in events organizing and cultural educational pan INDIA, is a 26yrs old guy who recently has entered the digital platform of imprinting emotions. He has initiated with his own open mic platform to help budding poets and aspiring writers under his brand named as "Teekhe Zasbaaat"

He is a commerce graduate from the Bhagalpur City of Bihar. He states Writing has impersonated him since childhood and he has now been writing for over a decade!

Cooking, on the other hand, is his passion! He also mentions, trying out new things just tickles him!

When asked sir, Why SPICY EMOTIONS?

He smiled and added, "agar jasbaat teekhe na ho toh wo jasbaat kahan" Spices are all that blends! So do his words!

As a chef, he presents to you his dish! Hot and freshly served! Taste it! Feel it! Enjoy it! You can also find his writing in the Book "Teekhe Zasbaaat" and 50+ Co -authored anthologies. With his passion to explore opportunities across Platforms, he is working with keen dev otion and We wish him all the very best for his future ventures.

He is Featured in the International Magazine DeMode for his upcoming solo novel.

He is Approved by Ne8x for its Lit Fest, and is a Golden Star Awards 2020 Winner.

He is a India Book of Records Holder for his Anthology Satrang, and has the Grandmaster title by Asia Book of Records, for the same.

He has also been featured in Prabhat Khabar, Dainik Jagran, and a lot of other Newspapers in Bihar for his achievements.

He has been a proud co-author to

India Book Of Records (Title- Black)

World Book Of Records (Title -15 Wonders of Poetries)

India Book Of Records (Title - Aaina)

Vajra World Records Holder (Title - Gustakhi Maaf Hai)

High Range of Records Holder (Title - Gustakhi Maaf Hai)

Indian Book of Records

(Title - Road from Worst to Best)

Share your reviews on his

INSTAGRAM

@spicy_emotions
@shubham4shah

Or via email on

shubham2shah@gmail.com

To stay tuned to his work and opportunities follow his business Handles

INSTAGRAM   FACEBOOK   YOUTUBE

@flairsandglairs
@teekhezasbaaat

WEBSITE:

https://flairsandglairs.in/
https://flairsandglairs.com/

Ishani Agarwal

(Co-Founder- Flairs and Glairs)

Ishani Agarwal hails from the City of Joy, Kolkata.
She is the co -founder of her Community "Teekhe Zasbaaat" and Flairs and Glairs Publication.
Been a Compiler for 45+ Anthologies, she is in the process for more. Co-authored in 150+ Anthologies. She is a India Book of Records Holder, a Vajra World Records Holder, a High Range of Records Holder, an OMG Book of Records Holder, a Bravo Record holder, a Forever Star Book of World Records and an Indian Book of Records Holder.
Approved by Ne8x for its Lit Fest 2020, and Literary Icon 2020. Also a Golden Star Awards Winner 2020.
She has also been award ed with India Star Republic Award 2021, a part of She Awards by Awards Arc and Winner of Nari Samman 2021 by Literoma.

She is also selected as Best Achiever of the Year by AwardsArc and Most Challenging Compiler Award by Spectrum Awards.
She got her first solo Published,a solo Compilation consisting of first 750 contents of hers, titled "Hand That Burnt While Healing".

She has been featured by the National Magazine "Taree Zameen Par" with the title 'unstoppable'.
Also featured in the International Magazine DeMode for her upcoming solo novel, she is proud to write on social issues, and is happy with the love she is receiving.
Connect with her on Instagram: @Ishani_agarwal_quotes / @compilations_so_far

Dr. Lavnya Krishnamurthy
(Compiler)

Dr. Lavnya Krishnamurthy is a doctor (Ophthalmologist) by profession and a writer by passion. She is also an avid reader, foodie and till her last breath, a die-hard Potterhead. She hails from the picturesque city of Coimbatore nestled in the foothills of the Western ghats. She has to her credit her first published novel, 'I Prescribe Love' released last year by Leadstart publishers. She has also co -authored an anthology titled 'Narratives in Monochrome', released recently by Flairs and Glairs publishers. She ardently believes that 'Words are the most inexhaustible source of magic', and strives to heal the world, one eye at a time. This collection of stories aptly titled 'Lockdown chronicles', has been compiled by her during the second COVID lockdown of May 2021.

She can be reached at:
Instagram handle: Eyedoc_writer_lavnyakrish
The story below has been penned by her father Dr. S.R Krishnamurthy, a practising onco -surgeon from Coimbatore, from whom she inherited her passion for medicine as well as writing.

The Covid Murder

"Dr. Sharmila, can you meet me immediately?" asked her HOD Dr. Pranesh at the other end of the line. Sharmila w as a young doctor who had recently joined as a junior consultant in a corporate hospital, and was on COVID duty. She noted from the tone of his voice that he sounded disturbed, and wondered whether she would get an answer to the question which had been plaguing her since the past two days.

"Yes sir, but I need to report to duty at 10 AM," she replied.

"It's only 9.15 AM now, you can first meet me then report for duty. This is urgent."

Gulping down her breakfast at the hospital canteen, she rushed.

HOD Dr. Pranesh was a tall, medium-built, pleasant-faced and a stylishly well-dressed person. As she entered his cabin, she noticed that the Regional medical officer Dr. Mathesh was also seated with him. They offered her a seat which she politely declined, preferring to stand. Then, warily looking around, Dr. Pranesh instructed his secretary to close the door and not let anyone in.

"Whatever you told us regarding that patient Mr. Manoj, needs to remain a secret, for your own safety and for the sake of the hospital's reputation," Dr. Mathesh said sternly.

"I'm saying this like a father to you- you are a brilliant student with her whole life and career ahead. Forget about all this and focus on your career and future," added Dr. Pranesh.

Sharmila's mind was turbulent on her way back to hostel, after this meeting with her seniors. She wondered why, instead of taking the appropriate action towards what she had reported, they had counselled her to keep quiet and given her three days off from work. How could they hush up the   truth- that there had been a murder attempt on patient Manoj?

She recalled that patient Mr. Manoj had been admitted during her duty, six days ago, with severe breathlessness. On account of his fever, high heartrate, low oxygen saturation, congested lungs and CT scan findings, she had diagnosed him to be a COVID patient. She had promptly started him on nasal oxygen and antibiotics. She had informed regarding a possible bad prognosis, due to the severity of the CT scan findings, to the patient's son. He however, had no reaction on his face to the news. On the second day, Manoj started improving and his oxygen levels were picking up. Joyous that her treatment had worked, Sharmila decided to taper down the nasal oxygen to four litres per minute.

On the fourth day however, he again deteriorated, with oxygen levels plummeting. A puzzled Sharmila increased the oxygen flow to ten litres per minute. A quick physical examination and a scan revealed that the condition of his lungs hadn't worsened. She wondered what the reason for his decline could be then. She regretfully informed the son that his father may not survive much longer. She was at that moment struck by the oddity of two things - the son's lack of a perceptible reaction once again and his closeness to the ward attendant Ramu. She also noticed that Ramu lingered near Manoj's bed more often and longer than necessary. Suspicious, she questioned him. "Madam, there are many patients waiting outside for beds, which won't be available to them unless some admitted patient dies," he stated bluntly the truth about the sad state of affairs. On enquiring with the duty -nurse that evening she came to know that the water in the oxygen circuit had been changed at 7.50 AM by the ward attendant Ramu. She realized with alarm that the patient had started worsening after that, at 8 AM. On lifting the oxygen mask over the patient's face, she realized that there was no oxygen flowing through it. She instructed the nurse to quickly change the oxygen cylinder and mask, following which the oxygen levels started improving. She then noticed a panicky Ramu trying to dismantle the entire apparatus, and stopped him with the help of her colleague Dr. Prem. Observing the unit that they had just replaced, they now noticed that a hole had been mad e purposefully on the cap of the bottle of water, which connected the oxygen cylinder to the mask. This had been causing a part of the oxygen to leak out, before reaching the patient. Also, the 'water' in the circuit looked and smelt like Kerosene. The pat ient's son confessed to having tampered with the same by adding impurities. After sending a sample of the water to the hospital's lab for testing, she had reported this matter to her HOD. But he had, as we saw previously, instructed her to keep quiet about it.

The one silver lining for her had been the fact that Manoj had recovered, subsequently.

A few days later, after her three-day-forced leave, much to her relief, she came to know that the hospital authorities had discreetly informed law enforcement and the culprits had been apprehended.

Prabal Tandon
(Compiler)

Prabal Tandon is a CA_Intermediate studentwho aspires to be a Chartered Accountant. He has many interests which include writing (quotes, poetry) on all topics. He also loves reading books, reviewing and writing blogs. This is the first time that he is working as a co - compiler, for this book. He   is from Kanpur (Uttar Pradesh). Kanpur is the main city of the state and the centre of industrial activities. He can be reached at:
Blog: booksloverprabal.wordpress.com
Instagram handle: iamprabaltandon
Facebook: iamprabaltandon

Dr. Urvashi Tandon

Urvashi Tandon is a Professor of Anaesthesiology who served in the INDIAN NAVY for 29 years. She is based in Gurugram and has written short stories for anthologies as well as articles for various magazines. She was one of 25 winners of a short story writing contest for women writers of India, held by eShe magazine which culminated in a book titled "Everything Changed After That". She has authored a book for children titled "Potpourri, stories for children" which is an illustrated book comprising a collection of 10 short stories aimed at increasing environmental awareness in children. Having worked as a Paediatric Anaesthesiologist, she is naturally inclined towards writing for children. She finds them impressionable and malleable. Being the future of any society, she believes that the right literary content could help in shaping a better tomorrow.

Just Another Day In The Times Of Covid

Surabhi unlocked the apartment door and sighed as she entered. She put down her bags of groceries and fresh veggies. It did seem strange as she shopped earlier at the supermarket. It had seemed like eons since she had last done her weekly shopping in that familiar manner. The last year had virtually flown by with doorstep deliveries and hardly stepping out of the apartment.

Had it really been that long?

As she sorted her weeks purchases, she reflected on the past one year. Surabhi and Gautam were childhood sweethearts. Their romance started with a very innocent fondness for each other in class V which gradually blossomed int o a full-blown romance as the years went by. They remained in touch while he pursued a rigorous course in medical college, and she went on to do Masters in business administration. Their families knew of course, and it was only in January last year that th e two of them had finally tied the knot. A brief getaway in the mountains was followed by getting back to work as Gautam was a Senior Resident in Medicine at a busy hospital. They had decided to shelve their honeymoon for later.

Precisely two months later, their lives changed completely as the first wave of the Covid -19 pandemic swept across the country. Gautam virtually moved out of their apartment and into the hospital He did not want to come home and expose her to any infection that he might carry. Sura bhi started working from home as the virus wreaked havoc in office spaces too. Domestic help was done away with and Surabhi hoped and prayed that these difficult days would pass soon. Video calls with Gautam were short and snatched at mealtimes , or when he took a quick break. She would send him changes of clothes for a couple of weeks but then even that stopped as he settled down into the doctor's hostel where all the resident doctors were staying. It did get rather lonely all by herself in the apartment.

About six months down the line, life seemed to be slowly limping back to normal in the outside world, when the virus struck closer home. Gautam had caught the infection and was admitted to the very same covid ward where he had spent hours on duty, Surabhi recalled as pulled out packets of pulses and stored them. Four days later, the video calls decreased as he was shifted to the ICU where he was breathless most of the time. She had panicked, not knowing what to do and how to reach out to him. He began to se nd her text messages instead of video calls as speaking was an effort. She pleaded with him for a video call, promising not to speak. There was this insatiable need to see him. Since she was not allowed into the ward, nor was leaving home advisable, a vide o call was the only way to satisfy her but, Gautam did not agree. He probably did not want her to see him in that state. She fought back her tears as she washed the vegetables before drying them out and putting them into the fridge. Memories of that fatefu l day caused the tears to overflow, blurring her vision as she vigorously rubbed the carrots. There was a call from Gautam, only it was not his voice at the other end of the line.

"Ma'am, this is Dr Prakash, a junior colleague of Dr Gautam's. I regret to inform you that he could not fight the virus. He tried hard Ma'am. I am so sorry".

She turned off the tap and sank to the floor as her body was racked with sobs. She stayed there for a good half hour before the phone's ringing caught her attention. Pullin g herself together, she reached for it and realized her mother was calling to check on her. It was nine months since her life seemed to crumble about her, but the pain was just as intense. She had heard it said that time healed everything but, this crushing pain inside her chest seemed to defy the norm. She wiped her tears and answered the phone as routine life took over for the time being.

Sudiksha Choudhury

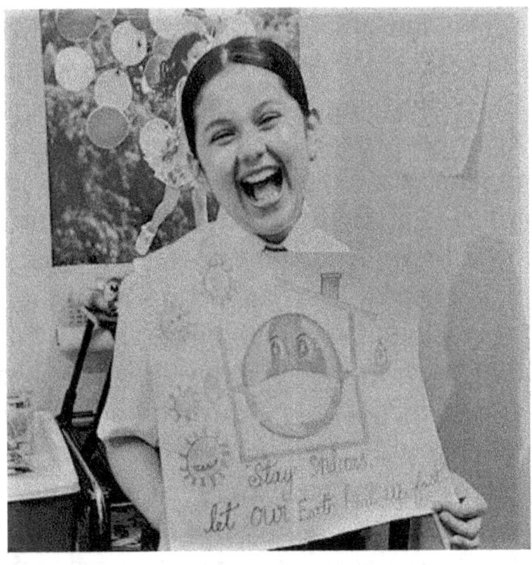

Sudiksha Choudhury is a fourth -grade student from Kolkata. She is 9 years and loves writing and drawing. When not busy with studies, she enjoys playing games on her iPad. She also maintains a diary that has a lock where she writes all her secrets. In this feature, Sudiksha chronicles her experiences in dealing with the pandemic and how it affected her life.

Online Blues

There was a time, not so long ago when I had to wake up early in the morning and get ready for school. Along came the pandemic and everything went online. After some time, I started missing my friends and all the fun we   had in school. Since my grandma was alone in Kolkata, my parents decided that we return to India from the US, and I continue schooling from there. I was overjoyed at the prospect of returning home, but my parents started to worry about my admissions. I was not so sure of cracking the admission tests since I did not know Hindi. I mean I knew it, but not too well. My dad got busy making all arrangements for our travel and finally the day arrived when we boarded the flight from the Newark airport. We arrived in Delhi, tired and exhausted. After we deboarded, completed the formalities and were about to make an exit from the airport, I suddenly heard some noise. A few policemen were approaching us. One of them said they were taking us away for questioning since we had submitted fake test reports. I felt a nudge. It was my mother.

"Hey, wake up. How long you are going to sleep? We have arrived."

I woke up with a start, realizing I was dreaming. Everything went well after that, and we finally took our next flight   to Kolkata after a long wait. Once home, I finally got to lay my hand on my old things —my toys, games, and my old diary. I picked the diary and flipped through a few pages when my mother called and said I must study. This was a day after we arrived. I heard my mother talking to my dad over phone about getting forms for school admission. I could not get out of the house and all I did for the next few days was study, study, and study. I was terrified before the admission test thinking what I would do. I tried my best and wrote whatever I knew.

When the phone call from the school came in a few days later, I was relieved. I was selected. A new life started as I got new books, dresses, and shoes. But everything was online once again. Life was no different than w hat it was in America. I started school and enjoyed what I learned, including Hindi — the one subject I dreaded. Slowly things started falling into place. I made new friends, but once again, they were all online. I wonder how long it would be before I can become a carefree child once again— going out for ice creams and playing with friends. I spend a lot of time by myself, playing games alone or drawing something. And every now and then, I dream of the life I once had when everything was not online. I just h ope things change soon and we get back to our lives —the way it was before the pandemic , a world where not everything was online

Sandeep Bhadange

Sandeep is a regular employee in the field of IT and is working with an MNC. His debut sci -fi novel "Howazzatt!?" has won rave reviews. Being an avid sports lover, he was able to set a vivid premise of Artificial Intelligence taking over the sport of Cricket, which eventually leads to the epic Cricket match between AI and Humans in the climax sequence. Sandeep also loves to write short essays that brings various human relationships in the foreground.

A Lesson In Shakespeare

"Anshu, Anshu! Wherefore art thou Anshu?"
Miss D'Souza always taunted when my webcam was off, fully aware that I hated Shake speare. During classes, my webcam switched off was on purpose. My horrible grades and resulting head shakes, taunts and pity from my classmates hurt. My only true companion barring the 'F''s in my tests had been Miss D'Souza, my English teacher. Webcam was fine during our chat sessions in the evening. Earlier in the term, we could chat after the school. However, since the pandemic set in, the world was locked-up. My life was saved by technology as we started connecting online every evening, with one strict rule though, 'no teaching'. With Miss D'Souza, I could talk my heart out. As for studies, she would send me the homework over an email marked as 'For Anshu to learn'. If the topic was difficult, she would add a smiley at the end, which was a cute warning.
"What is the girl's name?" Miss D'Souza asked unexpectedly one day.
"I don't know…" I stammered embarrassingly, wondering "How did she know???"
"But then, what's in a name? A rose by any other name would smell as sweet!" Miss D'Souza could always invoke a smile from me.
"She is the only one who doesn't mock me…I think her name is Juhi…" I started before a crashing sound interrupted us.
"I have to leave, M a'am!" I exclaimed and dropped from the video-call. Shivering, I quietly curled into my bed unt il the screaming and shouting had ceased. Like always, I opened the door of my room and quietly wrapped my arms around my bruised mother. My drunk father was lying in his room unconscious. My grades only got worse since dad had taken to gambling. Usually, I had to console my crying mother, but today she was uncomfortably silent. That night, I grabbed her

and ran out of that hell in the middle of a country-wide lockdown. We ran on foot into the pitch darkness, through the lanes that had been laid siege to by a dreaded disease. Dying to Covid-19 with dignity was better than dying at the hands of a monster daily. I knocked the door of my grandmother, who sheltered us.

"Cowards die many times before their death, the valiant never tastes death but once." Miss D'Souza soothed me in her own way upon learning the story next day. I wanted to talk much more but Miss D'Souza was in a rush. "You have a big test coming up next week," she said. "Forget everything else and focus on it. Whether we can continue talking in the evenings henceforth will depend upon you" I couldn't believe it! Was she threatening to never speak again upon my bad results? That's harsh!

"You may choose, loser or a winner. Your choice" Miss D'Souza spoke before hanging up. With no choice, I threw myself into studying everything, except that Shakespeare, of course.

Next day, our Principal M a'am made an appearance during Miss D'Souza's class. "It is unfortunate that Miss D'Souza has tested positive for Covid-19 and been moved to ICU last night. I will be filling her place until her return. She has already setup the upcoming test questions ," she declared. Until someone close is involved, the reaper remains unnoticed. I could feel the coldness of death around me. The only thing that had ever made sense in my life was Miss D' Souza. My impulsive rush to the door was arrested by the realization of the lockdown outside. When the big test started, the test paper shocked me. Five out of the total ten questions were about Shakespeare! Was it a cruel joke tha t Miss D' Souza was playing on me? I wanted to quit the test right away. But Miss D'Souza's words rang in my ears. "You may choose, loser or a winner". I took a deep breath and started attempting the questions. Surprisingly, I was able answer the most compl ex questions

on Shakespeare. It dawned upon me that during our evening chats, Miss D'Souza had been casually slipping in topics related to Shakespeare into our conversations. She had converted an unsuspecting foe of Shakespeare into his friend through her sheer genius.

"It is with great sorrow that I inform you that Miss D' Souza has lost her battle" Principal M a'am announced tearfully the next day. I had never felt so much emptiness in my being before or ever since. I lost all my senses to numbness at once for some time. "Anshu!" Principal Ma'am called me out. The entire class had left the meeting while I reeled from the shock. "Miss D' Souza was holding a print -out of your test paper when she passed away," Principal Ma'am said. "I am sending you a copy." Tears breached the gates of my eyes as I saw my test paper marked with a B+.

"Was she trying to tell you something?" Principal Ma'am inquired pointing to a red circle on my paper.

"No" I choked. "As usual, she was trying to teach me ." Miss D'Souza had marked the following part of my answer in red:

"All the world's a stage, and all the men and women merely players. They have their exits and their entrances; And one man in his time plays many parts". She had written 'For Anshu to learn' and put a smiley beside it.

"Romeo, Romeo! Wherefore art thou Romeo?" Juhi broke my train of thoughts. "Are we meeting in the evening or shall I kill thou?"

"Absolutely!" I remarked. "Frailty, thy name is woman!" As Juhi cracked up and waved me good -bye, my eyes fell upon the fram ed test paper on the wall. I spoke to it whenever I wanted to talk to Miss D'Souza about anything, including Shakespeare! Truth is, I could have easily gone the loser way. An angel made me realize that it was my choice who I wanted to be. After all, in the   end, to be or not to be: that is the question, isn't it?

Sugapriya Rajesh

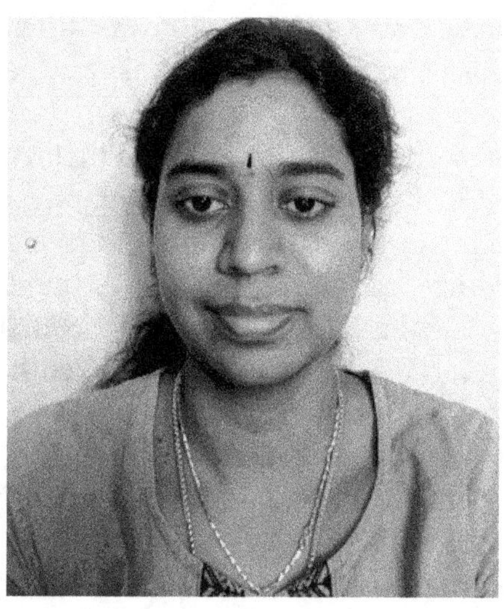

Sugapriya Rajesh is an IT professional and a published author. She writes short stories and novels. Her published works include Two Friends Meet over a Cup of Tea, Will Love ever Crumble? The Oscillating Mind! and The Daffles Series. She likes philosophy. Also, she has a strong passion for technology and artificial intelligence. Her stories mostly involve either philosophy or technology. She lives in Chennai, India with her family.

A Blessing In Disguise

The bright sun peeped out of the curtain, gazed at my face, and wished me good morning. I lazily opened my eyes and stretched. I looked eagerly at the mirror to check if a new adult tooth had started to peek through the   gap that was left by a milk tooth a few days ago. I could see a small, white -colored entity coming out of the gums. 'A new milestone for a 6-year-old boy! I thought with pride.'
I glanced at the Spiderman wallpaper across the walls of my room on which hung a Mickey Mouse clock and its small hand pointed to 9. All of a sudden, I felt a knot in my stomach. I yanked my bed sheet and got down hastily from the bed. My fairy would leave me soon. I will have to hurry up. I ran downstairs. I knew she would leave me any moment and I will have to spend the rest of my day with the monster. A giant monster with crooked teeth!
My eyes were already wet with grief as I had missed some of the valuable moments of the day having woken up late.
I instantly stopped with a jerk when I saw my fairy sitting on a couch and talking over the phone. I couldn't believe my eyes. I observed keenly how her mouth and lips moved to bring out the words. I tried to similarly move my lips but nothing came out. No matter how hard I tried, I cou ldn't hear any sound. I wished I could also speak like everyone. But I couldn't because of the agonies caused by the monster.
I noticed her wearing a casual dress. She seemed relaxed which was quite unusual in the mornings. I had a glimpse of her lunch bag which was empty and unpacked. My heart skipped a bit knowing she was on leave today. The very thought made me show all my teeth.
The doorbell rang and my fairy opened the door. The monster stepped in. I could feel the blood rush to my face. I hid behind

my fairy hoping she would save me. But she hasn't come to my rescue till now. I was in the dark.

The giant monster has covered her mouth and nose with something weird. I have seen people on the road wearing it these days. I didn't know what it was called.

"Ma'am, aren't you ready for the office?" queried Swarna.

"No Swarna, we don't need to go to the office from today. There is a lockdown announced by the government due to this pandemic situation. So, we will have to work from home, and I feel you needn't come here anymore," said Swapna firmly.

"I... I will be cautious and will take necessary precautions...," stammered Swarna.

"Sorry Swarna, we do not want to take any risk," said Swapna sternly.

Swarna left the house disappointed. I watched her leave t he house.

"Kanna! Are you feeling sad that you will be missing your Nanny? Don't worry, myself and Dad will be there with you. We will be working from home, and I will be playing with you as well," smiled my fairy.

I smiled back perplexed. I heard my fairy talking to my dad.

"Ranjan, did you get the doctor's appointment for Rohan?"

"Nope, it's difficult in this pandemic situation. Will try to get it soon. Is there any improvement from his side?" queried Ranjan.

"Hmmm... no... but he will get well soon," sai d my fairy, lost in her thoughts. I could feel her anguish. Her eyes expressed intense remorse.

Later, I heard my fairy yell, "Kanna, come and have your breakfast. What are you doing there sitting all alone?"

Being alone was not new to me. It was my famili ar world. A few minutes later, my fairy came and sat beside me. She took a piece of idli and put it in my mouth. I was waiting for this moment for a very long time. My eyes were filled with tears. I hugged her tight. I wanted my fairy to always be with me.

Every day, I have been eagerly waiting for the sun to set, the moon to appear and the stars to twinkle as these were the good omens for my fairy to appear. This wait has never ended till now. But I wanted it to end! I wanted it to end once and for all. My fairy has told me stories of great epics and we have enacted various roles in them. We played, giggled, and cooked together and have also created many things like a Spiderman toy, a six-wheeled car, and a birthday cake with Play-Doh. She read Panchatantra stories to me at bedtime. She has done everything to keep me happy.

My legs involuntarily climbed upstairs and moved towards the balcony. It was my regular practice for the past 3 years. I sat on the swing watching the happenings in the surroundings. I couldn't believe that I could freely move today as I was not allowed by the monster till today. Her rules were very strict. I could come down only to eat. During other times, I was asked to sit in the swing with my hands folded in front. I was allowed to play only with a few toys of her choice. The milkshakes and juices prepared specially for me by my fairy were only a treat to my eyes. The monster would make me clean utensils that were huge for my little fingers. I was allowed to enjoy the chillness of the a ir-conditioned room only when I cleaned it. The monster hit me with the wooden stick each time I disobeyed her. I wish I would have told everything to my fairy. But she threatened me not to tell anyone with an even bigger stick. I wept and wept for days. I t was hell on Earth. I prayed to God to rescue me from this monster.

The days passed.

I was still with my fairy. It had been days since I saw the monster. It was like a dream come true. I finally found the deprived love from my fairy, found a way out from the dreadful life, and enjoyed real freedom. I could sense a lot of positive changes in myself. I couldn't believe that God had answered my prayers.

After a few more days, I saw the monster again. She was standing with the same big wooden stick. She was la   ughing hysterically.

"My child! Did you think you were rescued? Nope! Never in your dreams!"

"You are born to be enslaved by me," laughed the monster. The monster dragged me into the dark.

Not knowing where I am, I was all drenched with sweat. I could feel a lump in my throat. I cleared it. I wanted my fairy to rescue me at least now. I wished I could scream at the top of my voice. I tried hard. My mouth went dry. I made weird sounds. Finally, it came out. The most beautiful word came out of my mouth. I shouted "Amma!" My fairy who was sleeping beside me, woke up, a bit surprised and a bit euphoric, hearing me scream "Amma!" She told me to repeat it over and over. She couldn't believe it! I was drenched in her pool of tears. Finally, I was able to speak and   was able to shout like other children.

I then realized that the monster coming back was just a dream and I was safe once for all with my fairy.

Namrata Naresh

She is the author behind the book 'Abhaya'. As a Human Centric Design Specialist with an advertising background, she realizes the power of story -telling. Have spent 20 years creating campaigns for various clients, she has been helping them to communicate and create a bond between the storyteller and the listener. Namrata can be caught reading a book, either a paperback or an e -book. Writing a novel has been on her mind. Eventually, with 'Abhaya – The Story of a Fearlessly Incandescent Girl', it has become a reality.When not absorbed in any gripping page -turner, she spends far too much time on her laptop. Namrata loves cooking, talking to friends, painting, travelling to new places. She lives in Mumbai with her family. To get updates on forthcoming books and stories, send an email to author@namratanaresh.com with the subject line: FICTION READER and you will be added to the special mailing list.

You can message her on any of the social media platform.
Facebook: https://www.facebook.com/namrata.naresh/
Instagram: https://instagram.com/namratanaresh
Twitter: https://twitter.com/NareshNamrata

Unleash The Hero

Emotions of the entire nation were running high as all waited for the Prime Minister, Mr. Narendra Modi, to address the country on television. An air of uncertainty also loomed over the Sharma's residence as Pravin, his mother, Mrs. Komal Sharma, two children Aditya and Nitya sat on the couch while Anu, Pravin's wife, was busy sanitizing the groceries that were delivered earlier.

The news blared on the TV set, capable of making itself heard by Anu in the kitchen. Every family had some apprehensions and judgements of the government's next steps to curb the spread of COVID -19 as there were many people worldwide losing their lives daily. India still had about 500 cases.

"I am announcing a 21-day lockdown of the entire nation, from tonight 24th March 2020," said Modi Ji. This made Anu drop her chores and come running to the living room. The shock was apparent on all their faces. The fate of millions of families like theirs was sealed.

Pravin, a tour manager with Royal Tours & Travels, had not gone on any tour since December 2019. News circulated about the spread of the deadly virus worldwide through the media. Spending time travelling on one tour after another for many years, Pravin had welcomed the short break. Anu worked as a junior assistant chef at "La Crème", a fine dining Indo-Italian restaurant.

Pravin's mother asked him what it mean t, while the children asked him when they would return to school. Anu stood there frozen, staring at Pravin in shock as she knew that the worst would hit their family in the days to come.

Guessing the outcome of the lockdown, Pravin tried reaching out to his family, friends, clients from past tours to help him get a job. With no positive result, Pravin opened a   bottle of whiskey gifted to him by a client during a tour to London. He

settled down to drink from it on the balcony to avoid Anu's and his mother's eyes.

By the morning, Anu too had received a call from the restaurant manager informing her that she was la   id off. Of course, protesting didn't help as she was somewhere expecting this to happen. But what needed her attention the most was Pravin and her family. She needed to pull him out from these dark shadows that were now hanging over their family.

Times like these remind us that life is hard but not bad. A hard life equalled to a life full of obstacles and challenging moments and also full of people you loved and cared about. It was time to turn things around. Anu spoke to her friends from the catering college without any outcome. Talking to her friend, Veena gave her the idea of starting a home chef business. Mentally deciding to do it, she sat and wrote down a small business plan to provide it with a direction. Writing it down made it easier as she realized the hurdles that she would face. The lunch meal had to be delivered to people within a 5km radius of her house. Spending a couple of hours to crack it and unable to do so, she approached a now sober Pravin telling him about her plan. Unable to read him, he said, "What do you think we should do?" Mulling over it, he said, "The only people I think can help us to deliver these tiffins are the newspaper delivery boys. They will also be out of jobs."

Excited that this could be something that could be worked out, she urged Pravin to speak to the newspaper distributor. The agency gave him the mobile number of three boys, Ramesh, Raju and Anand.

It was only one conversation with these boys that made Pravin realize their financial trouble. It was not only that they needed the boys' help, but this was a way for them to create a source of income for these three young boys and their families. Pravin realized that he too had a responsibility to fulfil and not leave it on Anu to handle this. He promised her that he would cooperate with her in every possible way.

The first step was to write down the weekly menu dictated by Anu to Pravin. This helped them make the grocery list that would be required for two weeks. Aditya and Nitya decided to help in their spare time after s chool. They were delegated the task of making the leaflets and giving them to Ramesh to be printed and distributed around. Pravin composed a WhatsApp message to share details of their business with family, friends, and people of their housing society.

Pravin handled the order booking; his mother helped with chores like cutting vegetables, etc. The children helped pack the meals once they were done with their school. It worked. The orders slowly and gradually moved from single -digit to double-digit orders.

Like any other day, the boys had come to pick up the meals. As always, Anu and the kids were standing along with Pravin handing them the meal bags. Even after they did, the delivery boys didn't leave. Not knowing how to breach the subject, Pravin persuaded them to share what was bothering them. Ramesh said, "Sahab, we noticed there are a lot of poor people in our vicinity. They are homeless and   have no food to eat also." Understanding what they were trying to say, Pravin said, "Ramesh, madam will prepare ext ra meals from tomorrow, and you all can distribute it to them."

"Thank you, Sahab!" they said sequentially and left.

Looking into Pravin's eyes, Anu said, "We are all so proud of you. I am glad you turned yourself around and did exactly what was needed. I love you, Pravin!" She hugged him tightly. The children and Pravin's mother joined for a group hug. COVID-19 has taught us to be resilient, be human again and feel what is happening around us. It has also taught our children and us to empathize with others and their situations, making us extend ourselves to help in whichever way possible. Unleash the Hero within YOU!

Rajiv Sharma

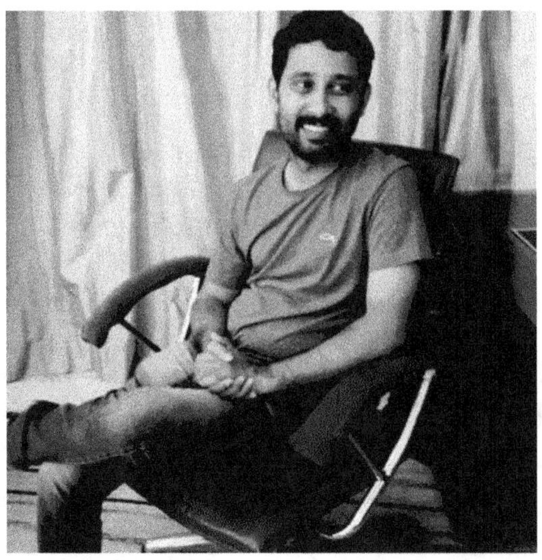

Rajiv Sharma is an engineering graduate working for a software firm based out of Bengaluru. His interest in writing started in school and he is a budding author. He has his passion in short stories, novels with specific interest in fiction, comedy and politics. He is inspired by writing styles of PG Wodehouse and Arundhati Roy. His writing style has a subtle take on the witty side imbibed in current political scenario.

Lockdown Blues

"Staying in big cities has its own merits," murmured my little neighbour Nithin, while packing up his stuff to leave to his hometown in Kerala.

There was no idea what condition his ance stral home back there would be, not to mention the numerous likeable things he would miss in his city – friends, quintessential weekend outings, favourite shows among others. But his dad and mom had made a decision, owing to the recent pandemic that looked seemingly like a girl's name.

"Mummy what if this corona reaches our house in Kerala also?" asked small Nithin still hopeful about staying back at his favourite place.

"We have better healthcare there," came the prompt response from his dad who was read y to drive the family off to safety. Being an avid news reader and strict taskmaster, it was his decision to go there. His neighbo urs were sceptical though, one of them even stating they (Nithin's family) were going to the place where the cases had been reported maximum.

True but his dad knew the difference between reporting the right numbers and not reporting at all. His travels had helped him and his calculations were to be proved right in another month. The main idea of controlling any pandemic is to judge and track the numbers. The people in Kerala seemed to get it correct somehow owing to their management of the deadly Nipah virus.

I always think if the same outbreak was there in any of the other states in India, the detection , tracking and finally containment would have taken a big toll. In most of the States of India big fanatism rules while in bigger ones Ram does. I had quickly decided to join them owing to the fact that I had a reasonable job and I coul d work from home if I could find Internet. Moreover, I would not be able to find food if a

lockdown was imposed in Bangalore, the city where we were staying. The idea that in Kerala we had the advantage of having independent houses as opposed to multi-storeyed flats struck a chord in me as well. Isolation at its best!

We were all set to leave when the Janata curfew for 24 hours came into force and also forced a change in our plans. I said to Nithin's dad "Laletta (etta being the short of Chettan meaning elder brother) I think we need to hire a taxi . I'm getting a hunch that this might extend."

He agreed and we frantically searched for outstation cabs on Ola and Uber to start immediately after the curfew. The curfew festival was celebrated well by my neighbo urs by clapping hands and beating on plates and some to the extent of lighting fireworks while we still were panicked that no taxi had responded to our SOS. I even tried out with my regular taxi services but to Kerala, they were s ceptical, the whole notion being that the epicentre of the virus lay there.

Finally, shortly after the curfew ended successfully and Corona had been fully driven out and many more burnt in the high temperatures prevalent in India, one Messiah responded. The driver Surya reminded me of the superstar in one of his most famous avatars and he indeed was one! I thought finally we are leaving the place where people are yet to understand that virus is not a living thing outside our cells. But then almost 90% of the people in India are virus illiterate, why blame certain commoners around? And finally, we reached there, our land of Canaan, feeling safe and happy. After all isn't it anything for happiness?

Dr. Anjali Kavthekar

Anjali is a practising Eye surgeon and a happy mom with a passion to serve the needy. She works in Tribal and rural areas in a mission to accomplish this desire of hers. An avid reader and observer, she loves to write her observations about life.

His First Vacation

"Maa, we are coming home, there is a   nationwide lockdown starting from tomorrow!" Abhinav said to his mother on phone.

Radha, his mother was happy with this news. Abhinav and Sneha, an IT professional couple were living away from hometown and were settled in the bustling city of Pune. Their parents Radha and Prakash never likedgoing there because for their whole li ves they lived in their old house surrounded by relatives, friends and helpful neighbours. Though they used to miss the kids and grandkids they never used to feel comfortable there. So occasionally they would visit and come back.

Prakash, a retired bank employee and Radha a retired school teacher lived a peaceful life. Prakash being the eldest son had responsibility of his family froma very young age as his father passed away and since then was working sincerely to make both ends meet. Gradually he got married, prospered and settled in Vadodara (Gujarat), got his two sisters married and took care of his aged parents. Now yes, he was free but during the golden years of life he and R   adha never really enjoyed anything as they were always busy with either work or some social responsibilities. Radha used to go to her parents' house during the summer holidays but Prakash never really had any vacation. Now when they were free the children   were busy. Yes, life was going on peacefully they never complained.

With the news of children coming home both of them geared up to make the house ready. Outside due to the news of lockdown there was lot of rush. Both of them went to supermarket and bought the daily essentials.

"Please take the car to a nearby toy shop. Let's buy something for the kids. Once shops are   closed, we are not going to get anything," Radha said. Lots of stuff was bought for the special guests.

Next day, Abhinav and Sneha came wit h their kids Shaurya and Shanaya. The house once quiet was now bustling with activities of kids, son and daughter in law and slowly their new schedule started. Every morning all of them would get up and get ready. Both Abhinav and Sneha would start working and take breaks in between . The kids loved being at their grandparents' home a lot and both of them became busy with gardening, cycling in the big openverandah, playing cards and board games with grandparents and with lots of stories from grandparents. Since there was lockdown , no guests came and no social activities were happening so for all of them it was blessing in disguise. They never really had this much quality time before and especially grandparents and grandkids were enjoying it to the fullest.

Abhinav and Sneha were more than happy with kids enjoying and letting them work and relax peacefully and especially with helping hands of both the parents . Every now and then they would start YouTube and make fancy dishes as kids wanted new dishes every time and everyone enjoyed.   Yes, grandparents were busy but very happy and having the satisfaction of lifetime. Many- a -times news came of someone close getting affected and even with slightest symptoms they used to feel anxious but family became their greatest strength and the positivity and precautions helped them to keep covid-19 at bay.

Finally, one day there was an announcement that lockdown is getting over.

"Maa, can we stay here little longer ? We loved it here ," the kids asked.

Abhinav and Sneha both were confused too as they were also very comfortable here. But what to do! Even if we love home a lot we have to move out and work. So yes, it was decide   d that they would leave by car the next day. Suddenly home was quiet and gloomy. Prakash was thinking,

"I enjoyed fully in my life for the first time- no worries about work, quality time with family especially the grandkids , lots of homemade food and no social responsibilities. This was the best time of my life   and first vacation which I have fully enjoyed. Though the place was home and not some exotic tourist place there was so much fun! Thanks to lockdown!! I feel bad for people who are badly affected by   this covid-19 pandemic but thanks to that lockdown I have enjoyed my first vacation!!"

The next day there was a call from Abhinav's company informing that they were planning to extend the work from home up to one year. Sneha also got the same news . So yes, when they informed the ir parents all of them were overjoyed with the news.

Indeed, this pandemic has given some invaluable moments and quality time. Every dark cloud has a silver line!

Sripremraj Sinnaiah

Sriprem is the co -founder of Wellness 96 Empire Pvt ltd, a wellness e-commerce startup based in Malaysia. He is a certified wellness coach, martial arts instructor, sports enthusiast and natural lifestyle practitioner. He actively pursues Varmakalai (ancient Indian martial art form) and Siddha (ancient Indian medical system) in his part time. He adores pets especially dogs are his favorite companions. He indulges in badminton, gardening and books during his free time. His lifetime goal is to create a holistic lifestyle model which can simultaneously improve people's wellbeing and revive mother nature through his ventures.

My Birthday Gift!!!

On my 32nd birthday my wife gifted me a Neem sapling. Yup I know it's hard to consider Neem tree for a present but it was rule which we went by (no fancy items or stuffs that can only serve as a memory, instead we choose things of monetary value like a FD or environmental value like a house plant). But a tree sapling was hard to accept given the fact that we were staying in an apartment at that time. Well , I am sure every married guy would agree on the consequences of a rejecting his wife's gift, it would be a self-inflicted disaster. Adding on I was a nature lover and so we decided we will find a way out for this plant. It was around 4 ft when she gifted it, by the 7th month it was 6 ft and growing faster than we expected. Luckily, we had a balcony where we had placed it . Initially I started with a pot then a bucket and towards 7th month I had to buy off a big drum to hold this tree. We were staying on 18th floor and I was already considering the possibility of my balcony cracking due to overweight. The load was quite along with my other indoor plant collection counting up to 30 pots. We were looking for options to donate the tree or find a public garden to plant it. But my mind was not letting it go and so started thinking of other alternatives. One fine day the idea of moving out of the house sparked in me and after further debate we decided to move into a landed house. With much efforts we moved into a landed unit with a small garden space. While deciding where to plant this neem tree, my mom strictly advised against planting a neem sapling within the house compound. So that left me with two options one right outside my gate was a small perch or across the road where we had enough area to plant a tree. For some reason I chose the perch and we planted it r ight outside our gate. This it grew up to a small tree of 15ft in 2 years. At times I used to contemplate the

consequences of my decision on holding onto the tree but always concluded that one day in future it would prove useful. Then came the COVID outbreak and all the disastrous events followed. It was during this lockdown my Neem tree became famous. Even though we had number of Neem trees in my area, either they were too tall or not easily accessible. Only mine was at the right height and it had visitors   almost every fortnight requesting for leaves. Neem leaves are a natural disinfectant and people needed those leaves to keep their environment safe from the virus. We were glad to help so many people and it was a feel-good thing for us. At end of the day, it was the best present I ever had for a birthday. Who would have thought that a birthday present would empower us to help people?

Next time when you plan to gift someone   , I would strongly suggest to think of something that might create value for the recipient rather than just a memory.

The above anecdote is one of my positive outlooks during this Lockdown.

Anubhav Bakshi

Anubhav Bakshi is an author and Blogger. His published works include Retribution - The Hunt for A Traitor, an edge of the seat spy thriller, and Gia and The Old Magician, a fantasy tale for Children. His blogs can be read at his website, www.anubhavbakshi.com. He works for an International Airline, and has travelled around the world gaining deep insights into the different cultures, and people. Through his stories he wants to entertain, as well as compel the readers to think about the inherent themes of his books.

A New Hope

"You are a very selfish man. All you care about is you an   d your work," said Priya as she stormed out of the room.

Rahul and Priya's relation ship was collapsing. The once inseparable couple, now could not even stay together in the same room without fighting. The fights were a constant occurrence. In the race to f ind a better and comfortable lifestyle for themselves, their love had taken a back seat. After the Lockdown was imposed by the government due to the Covid-19 pandemic, the workload for both of them had increased tremendously. The already fragile relationsh ip was now on the brink of breaking. And the different shifts made the matters worse. They hardly saw each other while living under the same roof. And whatever little time they spent together they were fighting.

After today's fight, Priya had had enough, a nd she was contemplating separation. To her eyes, Rahul had become an egocentric man who was only capable of thinking about himself. She decided to call her mom and convey her decision before she spoke to Rahul.

Just as Priya picked up the phone to call, t   he phone buzzed. She glanced at the screen to find that it was their maid Suman's call. Priya disconnected the call. But the phone buzzed again and again. Getting irritated and angry, she picked up the phone and shouted, "Suman! Why are you calling me again and again at 8 in the morning?"

Priya was going to scold her more but stopped as she heard Suman crying.

"What happened Suman? Is everything OK? Why are you crying?"

Suman spoke in a choking voice, "Didi, my husband Shravan passed away." And she again burst into tears.

"How? When?" Priya couldn't find words to make a sentence.

"He was infected with Covid, and last night he started complaining of breathlessness. I immediately called my neighbours, and they arranged for an ambulance to take him to the hospital. But by the time, it arrived, he was gone," said Suman while crying loudly.

"They even took his body, saying that it will be cremated by them. My kids couldn't even see their father for the last time."

"Suman! Control yourself. It is a tragedy butyou have to think about the kids."

"That's why I have to call you Didi. I have been forcibly admitted to the hospital because my report was also positive. My kids are all alone, no one is there to look after them. I didn't know who else to call. Please he lp me, Didi. Please do something for my kids," Suman pleaded.

"Don't worry Suman, I will take care of the children. I will immediately go to your house."

Disconnecting the call Priya rushed to the room where Rahul was working. But she stopped in her track s. She remembered the morning's fight and immediately realized that she had forgotten about the situation at home and she hadn't even spoken to Rahul before promising help to Suman.

But then the faces of Suman's children flashed before her eyes, and she slowly walked towards Rahul. Unsure how he would react, she explained the situation. Rahul didn't say anything and went into deep thought.

Disappointed, Priya was about to leave thinking she had made a mistake, and how she would explain to Suman, that he canot help her, just then she felt Rahul's had on hers.

"I've been thinking a lot since morning. I am planning to take some time off from work. I need a break. We both do. You should also apply for leave for 15 days."

Priya was confused.

Rahul smiled and said, "Two little guests would be coming to stay with us. How rude it would be of us if we don't spend time with them. Now quickly get ready. Let's get those kids home. They must be really scared."

A broad smile erupted on Priya's face, she tightly embraced Rahul.

Priya's phone buzzed again.

"Priya! I just saw your three missed calls. Is everything OK?

"Yes Maa, everything is fine. It's great. I will call you later," she said and once again fell into Rahul's open arms.

Deepa Ravi

Content writer & Communication strategist
Deepa Ravi is a copywriter and content writer who loves to dabble in different genres of writing. She has written and directed several plays for children and experimented with short stories, some of which have been published. She has also done story telling at birthday parties and other events. For her stories, she draws inspiration from the world around her and likes to keep her characters 'real and relatable'. Deepa lives in the heart of Chennai city with her family. Muchto her family's dismay, she is a great sucker for sob stories and is known to give away large donations to anyone who tells her their 'sad tale'. When she is not getting suckered or working or doing stuff around the house, she loves to chill with her daug hters - one a human, and the other a canine.

Unlocking Roles

"There is a lockdown on and you're telling me you don't know how to cook?" he said in anguish. "But I was told that you are a good cook…" He mutters "Yes ok. I lied about it. Well, technically my mom did ," Aditi sa ys wringing her mehendi adorned hands, while her new husband gape s at her. "You mean you can't cook ANYTHING?" he gasps.

"Umm I can keep rice. I'm very good at that. And…toast and stuff…" her voice fades as she catches his horrified expression. "Well, you should have married a cook then!" She exclaims angrily "If you marry a working girl, this is what you get ok. And… and what's with the inquisition? What about you? Can you cook? Can you do stuff around the house?" She says gathering steam.

"What do you mean… 'stuff around the house'?" he mimic s angrily. "You know, like fixing leaking faucets, changing lightbulbs, dusting cobwebs and stuff?" She challenges. "Why not? I'm sure if push comes to shove, I can do it ," he says shrugging. "Oh yeah?" she says, her voice dripping sarcasm . "What? You don't believe me huh?" He says, rolling his sleeves and challenging her . "Ok. Here's the challenge. You set right that leaky faucet in the bathroom and I make us dinner." She says, snapping her fingers. "You have to cook ok. No ordering from Swiggy," he warns.

"And you too. No getting any help from the UC app. DIY. Oh wait, of course you can't. There is a lockdown on ," she says contentedly, flipping her hair.

"Deal!" They say in unison "Well, our time starts now. We each have one hour to fix it ," she says and starts to walk towards the kitchen. He trots off to the bathroom. Thirty minutes later, the house is filled with the smell of something burning. He peeps out from the bathroom all w et and grimy. "Are you burning my house down?" He yells, his nose sniffling the air, as he runs towards the kitchen. "OMG! Look at you? What did you do? Fight a war with the faucet?" She exclaims looking at his bedraggled condition. "Ha Ha so funny. What's burning?" He asks peeping into the stove "YOU BURNT THE RICE?" he yells.

"Yeah well, I told you I can't cook ok   ," She says, looking mildly guilty, but then recovers fast, "Look now we're even, I can't cook and you can't be the repair man. Let's just call truce and order something nice for dinner," she says coyly. The new husband grins. "I'm actually looking forward to having my sweet wife for dessert," he says with a leer.She gets even more coy "Ok I'm gonna have a shower. Be with you in 30 minutes." She kisses his cheek and disappears into the bedroom. He surveys the mess in the kitchen, sighs, and starts to clean up.

Forty-five minutes later, she swishes out of the bedroom, smelling fresh and nice. She stops in surprise to see the house all dark, except for the candles.

"What happened here…oh wow…" She stops in her tracks as she sees the romantic setting on the dining table. Steaming hot rice and some nice smelling yellow gravy. Candles. Nice cutlery. "This is…nice. Did you order food then?"   She asks her beaming husband "No, my sweet wife. I cooked it. Simple, candle lit dinner of dhal and rice," says the still grimy husband, as he takes a bow. "Awesome! I'm impressed husband!" Aditi grins. "But I refuse to eat with you unless you clean up an   d wear something nice," She says eying him warily.

"You wish is my command my lady. Be with you in 10 minutes." He takes a mock bow and disappears into the bedroom. She settles into the living room couch and sighs with contentment. Ah how nice to have a hu sband who can cook, she thinks. He comes back, as promised in 10 minutes, smelling of some nice aftershave.

"Umm you smell nice husband." She flirts with him . "So do you, my love. By the way, you know the bathroom faucet, it

seems to have fixed itself. It' s not leaking anymore," he says happily. "Oh no. I fixed it ," she says casually . "You…you what?" He asks, taken aback. "I fixed the faucet and the bedroom light for that matter. She shrugs and then gets slightly miffed at his aghast expression. "What? Didyou actually think I was bathing for 45 minutes?" she challenges. "Oh boy! You have hidden depths that I need to discover ," he says as they settle in for their meal. Aditi giggles as she serves herself. Her husband gawks at her.

"Whatever happened to serving the husband and all that?" he asks teasingly "Why? You don't have hands to serve yourself?" She asks chomping her food. "Oh , this is so yummy. You're a good cook I say!" She compliments happily. They eat in companionable silence and then clean up together.

"So, it's fixed then! We know what each of us is good at. Plan the meal for this week and I will go out and get the stuff we need for it," she says running her fingers along his cheeks.

"When you do all this, I can only plan for one thing."He leers and grabs her hands.

"Ok look. Seriously, you can't drive. So let me do all the outside work. I suck at housework, but I promise to help you clean up and all. Let's accept each other's strengths and weaknesses. This way there will be peace."

"Yes, oh Lord and the Master ," says her husband bowing to her.

"Yes I am. And the sooner you realise that, the better it will be." She teases him.

"Oh, just you wait, let me show you who the master is ," he says lunging towards her. She squeals in delight and they both run into the bedroom.

Dr. Narendra Goel

Dr. Narendra Goel is a medical practitioner, a leading Child, and a new born specialist, practicing in NCR of India. Writing habit gradually grew upon him to take a shape of full -fledged blog, poem, and story writer. He hosts https://jabberingwanderer.com/ where he posts his experiences, views, and opinions on contemporary issues and his travel experiences. H is published works include " An Illustrated life" (Wolf Publications) and a travel diary 'Andamans' (Wattpad). Apart from writing, the author 's interest lies in gardening (best terrace garden ,2020), sports (being adjudged sportsmen of the year twice in successive years at IMA Ghaziabad sports awards), and watercolour painting. Dr. Narendra lives in Ghaziabad with his family.

Binoculars

How much TV can one watch in a day? Pinku , ten and by himself, one fine lockdown day, rummaging through the storage, found his binoculars, and a new pastime. Next two days he spent on the terrace. One evening, leaning on the parapet, he snooped on the houses and balconies curiously, which were on the farther range of the binoculars. Moving from the far east end of the row of houses, he saw people walking briskly on roof, men washing clothes in balcony, children playing on terrace etc. He got jaded soon. The next house in the row had the window open and the room was well illuminated. A couple was standing facing each other. They appeared to be amidst a heated argument. It soon escalated to a combat, and like trained boxers they circled each other with their faces close to each other, yelling. The altercation turned into physical blows. The man hit first, sending a slap across her face, and the woman retaliated by punching his face. Then the woman slumped on the sofa, sobbing, and the man walked out of the room. Pinku didn't have to wait for long, as the man reappeared, and threw himself on the sofa, clambering over the woman. She sprang to her feet quickly, but a little late, as the man raised his hands over his shoulder and stabbed her in the chest. The glint of the flashing blade appeared only for a moment during its arc, hitting the last few orange sun rays of the setting sun, but enough for Pinku to discern it as a knife. Pinku staggered, losing focus. On trying to re-focus, he could see neither the man nor the woman there. Rushing downstairs, Pinku grabbed his father's hand and dragged him to the terrace. Explaining was a more difficult task for him suddenly. "It looks as if you have seen a murder," Kuldeep, his father blurted. "Yes, I have seen a murder," Pinku said. It was not his words, but the look on his face which caused Kuldeep to ejaculate, "What? Where? When? Who?" Pinku dragged him to the same point, but found the window closed. "The house

belonged to my friend Shiv," Kuldeep dismayed. On one hand, Kuldeep was obliged to inform the police about the murder, on the other, he wasn't sure of what his son saw. He picked his phone and was about to call Shiv, but stopped abruptly. *What would he ask him* ? *"Hello, Shiv Good morning. Have you murdered your wife just now? "* This would sound preposterous. Having thought for a while, he still called Shiv's number. This was one of the phone calls when one hopes not to get picked. As a huge relief, it wasn't picked up. He didn't try again. Next morning with shaking hands, Kulde ep along with Pinku reached for Shiv's door bell. He was rehearsing the conversation in his mind furiously. Shiv appeared from behind it, flustered, holding a long knife in his hand. Just at that moment, Shiv lunged at Kuldeep and to shake hands   , came dangerously close, making Kuldeep tremble.

"Hey, sorry to keep you waiting. I was in the kitchen and listening to some music," Shiv said mockingly.

"I hope everything is okay," Kuldeep, white as a sheet, said looking beseechingly past Shiv.

"Of course. Why? So, what made you come to this place during this lock down?"

 "Nothing. Thought why not have a cup of tea with my friend" Kuldeep said sheepishly.

Clearly, any appetite for tea which he confessed was nowhere to be seen. Having seated both, Shiv went to th   e kitchen to prepare tea.

"Sugar?" He yelled from the kitchen. In answer, Kuldeep, with courage got up and sneaked into the kitchen silently and stood behind Shiv. By the time Shiv realized someone standing behind, and turned, Kuldeep had scanned the kitchen completely. *Nada. Nothing suspicious here.*

Tea was brought to the room , with Kuldeep walking behind Shiv, craning his neck around. Setting the cups at the table, Shiv went back into the kitchen to get some cookies. Kuldeep whispered something in Pinkus's ears and Pinku immediately sprung from his seat and went to the adjoining bedroom. When Shiv returned and asked about him, Kuldeep said, "Oh, he has gone to the washroom."

Inside the room, Pinku first opened the closet and found no corpse. Next, he fell on his knees and looked under the bed, nothing was there either. Quickly he slipped into the bathroom. Relieved Pinku came back and sat on his chair. His eyes met his father's, and conveyed that nothing amiss was there. "It has been a beautiful morning today. The pollution has drastically gone down in the last few days. Have you been to the terrace lately? Why can't we go to the terrace to sip our tea?" Kuldeep said suggestively. "Terrace is not clean," said Shiv defiantly.

"We will enjoy the weather ," Kuldeep was unrelenting. Without much waiting for the reply, Kuldeep stood, followed by Pinku, and started walking towards the stairs to the terrace. The terrace was indeed carpeted by thick dirt, making footprints wherever they walked. It took only a few seconds for Kuldeep to know that no one had walked on the terrace for ages. Barely a few seconds in the terrace, Kuldeep muttered. "I think it's dirty enough to walk. Let's go downstairs."

"Sure. As it suits you." Kuldeep was losing his patience now. Back in the room Kuldeep continued looking. "Where is your wife?" Kuldeep asked, looking intently at Shiv's face.

"She has gone to her mother's place."

"When?"

"Today morning."

How appropriate, Kuldeep thought. Pinku, a little bored of playing detective's sidekick, was starting to lose patience. He fidgeted first, then started touching nearby things. He was twiddling the media player on the side stool, when accidently he touched the play button. A ping sound came and the speaker on which the media player was sitting, suddenly started making a rumbling noise. Pinku was ta ken aback. Suddenly the room came alive and the wall behind the chair Kuldeep was sitting on, turned into a screen. Pretty large one. By program default the movie being played, rew ound to 30 seconds. It was an intense scene. A woman was sitting on a settee and a man with a knife lunged at her. Following Pinkus' wide-open gaze at the wall, Kuldeep too turned and saw this scene. Then they both looked at each other. The moment his blood shot eyes met Pinku's, the latter turned his face away. It would have been totally unnecessary to create a scene over here. They both stood up silently. Suddenly tea, manners, formalities and goodbyes were a thing of a faraway world. They both dashed out of the door.

All they could hear was Shiv's voice following them. "What happened?"

Pallavi Sharma

Pallavi Sharma was born in Nagercoil, Tamil Nadu on June 7, 2013. She is currently studying in third grade at Orchids International School Vivekananda, Sahakar Nagar, Bangalore. She is also getting trained in Taekwondo and has secured green-1 belt. Her interests include drawing, music and dancing in addition to reading and writing. Her mother's name is Mrs. Preetha and father's name is Mr. Shiva Prakash. She has one sibling named Baby Avyaan.

My Experiences During This Pandemic

All these years I was having fun at Bangalore. Because of the pandemic my school was closed. So, when my father and mother went to work, I used to be alone at my home in Bangalore. They did not want to leave me like that, so they thought of leaving me in my father's native place at Suchindrum [Kanyakumari district] in Tamil Nadu where we had a joint family. One day, while I was playing with my friends, they called me and told me to pack my bag. I had already told to my friends that I wi ll be going to my native place. I went to my room to pack my stuff, after which we ate dinner. Next day we woke up at 5 am and started our journey. My father drove the car, mother was   at his side and I was sleeping in the back seat. After a while I couldn' t sleep and started looking outside. We had breakfast in between in a hotel and continued our journey. I kept on asking , "Where did we reach father?" and he patiently explained. In between my grandmother called us to ask where we have reached. By that time, it was 4 pm.

Finally, after the long journey we reached home at 5 pm. We were happy seeing everyone at home including my aunt whom I call Ninamma and my cousin sister Neelu. My mother and father thought of staying for 2 days and then go back to Bangalore for their work. However, seeing my sadness, they extended their travel plans and very soon India came to a lockdown - March 24, 2020. In May my mother got a stomach pain and my father took her to a hospital. They came back with a very happy news that I was going to be a big sister. I was so happy to hear that. Before that in April, we had celebrated my mother's birthday with wheat cake. Ninamma had a friend named Surumiya who had a You-tube channel and she shared the recipe with us. We made the cake together. We played so many games during this lock down period including card games and outdoor games. On May 1st we celebrated sports

day with so many outdoor and indoor events. I got lot of first prizes. Other activities during the lockdown included regu lar quiz sessions, antakshari, dumb charades and treasure hunt in which all family members participated. My birthday was on June 7 and we celebrated it by cake cutting and I got lot of gifts. In between I did miss my Bangalore friends and I used to video c all them. The days passed by with happiness and sadness.

In September, my father and uncle had high fever. My father tested covid positive and went to hospital and next day my uncle also tested positive. Rest of us at home took the test and in that five pe ople including me tested positive. We went to the same private hospital where my father was admitted while my uncle went to a government hospital. Next day my mother also tested positive and was admitted in a room near to me. Many days later we all got dis charged and remained in strict room quarantine at home for the next one week. During room quarantine I saw movies and played lot of games with my uncle. My mother and father got discharged after few days. Navratri was nearing and after a week we started our Navratri preparations. We set up the kolu and I used to sing bhajans every day in front of the kolu. After that came Diwali and this years' Diwali was special with the arrival of my little brother. In December my father planned to leave myself, my mother and my little brother at my mother's place in Kerala and go to Bangalore to vacate our house.

At 31st December we got up at 6 am, got ready and bid goodbye. At 10 am we reached Haripad, which is in Alappuzha district in Kerala. I was so happy after the lo ng journey. My mother's sister, Veena was also there. Aunt Veena had a daughter named Amilia whom we call Amy. Amy and I became good friends. Another aunt named Remya had 2 daughters – Sowmya and Swapna. Sowmya was 9 years old and Swapna was 5. We became b est friends. My father came

from Bangalore in March and we left back to Suchindrum. We reached Tamil Nadu again and I felt happy.

April 14th was my mother's birthday which we celebrated by cutting a plum cake. Next lockdown has come – April 2021. Days passed by and on May 1st my happiest day approached – I got a cute puppy! We named it Snow white. In June, my birthday came and I was in a surprise. A kinemaster video with my friends wishing me and with my photos were released as a gift to me. Along with that I got cakes and gifts. It was a best day and I became 8 years old. Lockdown restrictions continues and we all have to be careful till the pandemic gets over. Stay home and stay safe. Thankyou.

Dr. Jyothsna Krishnamurthy

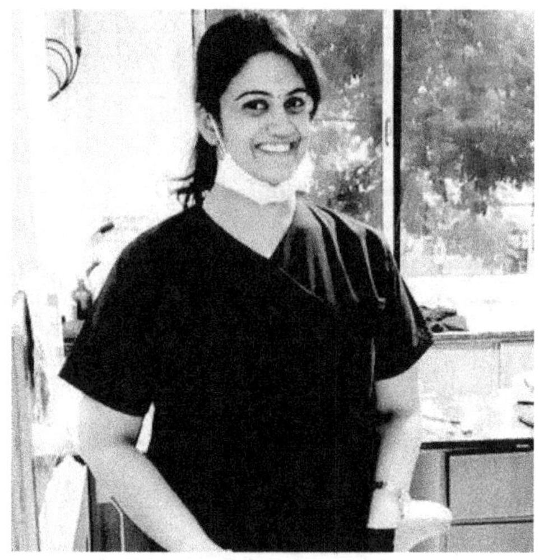

A dentist, dog-mom, potterhead, bibliophile, orophile, animal lover & PETA member from Coimbatore, Tamil Nadu, Dr. Jyothsna Krishnamurthy aspires to live her life by the quote "be the reason someone believes in the goodness of people." Also, as a first -time writer, she believes that words are an inexhaustible source of magic and hopes to spread hope, optimism and kindness, through the same.

The Covid Selfie

"Ow!" I shouted as my head bumped onto the roof of the tiny little cab that was hurtling through the narrow lanes   of some Keralite village. At this, my driver dove into what sounded like an explanation/ apology, in pure, unadulterated Malayalam, a beautiful language, but just one that I didn't follow, save for a few words here and there. I hadn't seen the point in honing my conversational skills in the said language, just for the sake of a two-week workshop. But those two weeks had dragged on to two more in my hotel room, thanks to the curfew.
Oh, I missed my family like hell. As tears pricked my eyes, the car jumped over another bump and jolted me back to reality, and my driver's enthusiastic monologue.
"Er…Oh…Umm…" were all the responses I could come up with, as he went on and on. Seeming to realize my illiteracy at his mother tongue, he thought hard and said "This is bad road. Two kilometers after, main road, good road" in the broken Tamil that he could manage.
"Thank you, anna ," I told and managed a very weak smile. True to his words, we soon turned onto a main road, albeit an empty one and started zooming towards our destination.
As we neared the Kochi airport, my phone chimed with a message from my airline that 'regretfully' all their flights were cancelled, indefinitely. Ignoring the feeling of panic seeping through me, I called the airport and asked them for the   next flight to Coimbatore, only to receive the answer that there were none for now.
Unable to believe my predicament and not ready to spend another day in a hotel room, I rushed through numerous probable solutions in my head, none of them plausible. Instinctively, I dialed my mom's number, but hung up the moment I imagined the panic and worry on her and Appa's faces. Through the tears that were incessantly flowing down

my cheeks and blurring my vision, I vaguely saw a sign board welcoming us to Kochi Intern ational Airport. Hastily, I told the driver to pull over and not enter the premises.

By then, the driver sensed my despair and asked me " What happened molae? What problem?" The look of concern on his face broke me even further, as I answered brokenly that my flight was cancelled and there was no way for me to go home. He remained silent for a few minutes, excused himself out of the car and started making calls.

As my mind started accepting the reality of the situation, the driver stepped back into the vehic le, and asked "Molae, no e-pass to Tamil Nadu, but I take you to the border, Walayar. From there, you have someone to take you home?"

At this, I just blinked, until the weight of his words sank into me.

"You'll drive me down to Walayar, in your car, just l ike that, now?" I asked, with strange hope and an ingrained fear bubbling within me.

Seeing my obvious fear, he gave me a small smile and said "Molae, I have daughter, your age. She is in college, Pune. She tried hard to come home, but no. Every day she calls my wife and cries," He broke off, with tears in his eyes, cleared his throat and said "I see you like my daughter. I will take you to Walayar safely. Here," He handed his Aadhaar card, license and a paper with his car details "take photo of all this and send to your parents. Ask at home and tell me ," Leaving me shocked and confused.

Unable to think anymore, I quickly dia lled my brother's number and explained the whole situation to him. After a few silent beats, he requested to speak to the driver. Over the speaker, I heard them converse in Malayalam, heard few names being passed around, and then my brother told me, "I'll be waiting for you in Walayar. I'll handle our parents. Don't worry about the money. Send me the driver's documents, stay awake, keep y our door unlocked and windows down. Send

your live location and call me every 30 minutes." With that the line went dead and I closed my eyes, sent a prayer to God and checked the Aadhaar card in my hand and said "Okay, Krishna anna, let's go."

For the next two hours, my mind and body exhaustively multitasked between checking google maps, calling my brother 4 times, answering my parents' call 8 times, answering the queries of the policemen who stopped us and having our temperatures recorded 6 times, conversing with Krishna Anna (alternating between my broken Malayalam and his broken Tamil) and praying to God in every language I could.

And before I realized, we had reached Walayar check -post. I could vaguely make out the outline of my brother walking towards us. In a few minutes, he and Krishna anna had explained our situation to the guards, and the latter started unloading my luggage, as he said "Molae, you can go home now."

My eyes blurred with tears of relief, gratitude and happiness "Thank you so much, anna. I…" I broke off. With a shrug, he said "Today I help someone's daughter home safely, tomorrow God will help my daughter."

Just then, my brother engulfed me in a bear hug and after a very teary reunion, he thanked Krishna anna profusely in Malayalam, and pressed a wad of cash into his protesting hands. "It might help your daughter come home ," I told, and he accepted it.

A few moments later, as my brother started to walk towards Tamil Nadu, with my luggage in tow, I stood at the border, and looked back at the man who had been my guardian angel.

'I should never forget his face. I should never forget the power of kindness and humanity ,' I thought to myself and ran back to the cab, "Krishna Anna, one selfie!"

Within few hours, my whole family and friends had seen the picture, of a tall, willowy, shy looking man standing next to me, and praised, blessed and prayed for him.

Dr. Suyog Vankudre

Dr. Suyog Vankudre, is an Organisation Development Coach, Trainer, Amazon Number One Bestselling Author, Motivational Public Speaker and recently won the awards for his client- "Best HR Strategy of the Year" & "CHRO of the Year" in Renewable Energy Industry. He has been in this field for more than 23 years, with exposure to 13 Industries while working with European, American, and Asian companies which were Industry leaders in their respective industries in the capacity of Strategy & HR Leader. As a strategic leader in many organizations, he has turn ed around the Employee Engagement Index, People Productivity by using effective HR strategies suiting as per need and addressing any organization-related issues from time to time.

LinkedIn:
https://www.linkedin.com/in/dr-suyog-v-a866548
Connect with the author at:
Facebook:
https://www.facebook.com/suyogvankudre
E-mail:
Suyogvankudre@gmail.com

Sam And His Grandpa's Story- "Lockdown: An Opportunity To Have A Dream Life And Gratitude For The Beautiful Life We Have."

Many years had passed since the COVID 19 impact. It was now a digital world . Sam was with his grandfather at the airport. While they waited for the flight, Sam asked his grandfather, "Hello Grandpa, will you share some life -changing experiences or difficult situations you have faced in life?" His grandpashared with him the experiences and memories of the lockdown he faced so many years ago. His grandfather replied, "Come, child, let me share with you the story of the COVID 19 impact and the lockdown situation. This lockdown has changed my life. As soon as the first lockdown was announced, many of my coaches, who were also in senior positions, such as CEO or MD, called me to ask me how to manage during the lockdown. For their reference, I shared various articles on a social media platform.

I personally foll owed the same recommendations which I had already given to them. Life during the lockdown was almost like a dream life, and we were fortunate to have that life. The goal was to live a more balanced life, which included spending quality time with family members, contributing to society with others or alone, focusing on inner peace, and managing a team. Some of my key achievements during and also because of the lockdown, which would have otherwise not been possible, I will share with you now.

I would never say that lockdowns a re good, as I know many people have suffered as a result of the same. However, some of my coaches insisted that I share this part with a large number of people, as we had noticed that many people had complained a lot about the lockdown, and we had many opportunities as an individual and as a team. As a result, rather than blaming the situation, it was time to focus on what we c ould control. There were many big companies, service providers such as "Zoom" that had grown like anything during that lockdown as they were

prepared for growth and accommodated all the requirements of the customers. I strongly feel that in such a situation, rather than blaming ourselves, we should focus on whatever is possible for us and try to make a contribution to our own and society's betterment.

The first thing I did was, I arranged food, groceries, for people who were genuinely in need of food, but found it awkward to ask for help, so I provided money to allow them to buy the items they needed without any promotional activity, preserving their dignity. The names of those people were never shared with anyone. I took advantage of the travelling time I saved, to establish myself as a writer. I published my first book, "Managing Work from Home", which has become Amaz on's #1 Bestseller. This book was part of my research work and I could share my research with many professionals with lots of case studies, tools, and guidelines. Finally, that book has given me Amazon's #1 bestseller tag. "

"Wow! Grandpa, that's interesti ng!" Sam was very vocal in his expression. "Lockdown meant that we were not supposed to move outside our house. I had enough time after office hours to write the book. Also, every evening and weekend, to contribute to the environment, I invited my friends to join me and we planted lots of trees and also took care of the same consistently. These trees are now flourishing. Due to our initiative, even the children in our premises are alert and take care of the plants personally. They don't damage plants but also ensure timely watering and the safety of plants. I noticed you and your friends watering the plants in scheduled manner. Keep doing good work!" Sam felt nice to know about his contribution also.

"I also encouraged my friends and made an arrangement for consistent drinking water provision for the vaccination centre, free of charge," his grandfather added. "I realized many people were interested in supporting this noble cause and I was getting repetitive calls from donors who wished to donate the water. I had to keep many donors on the waiting list as I already had great support from various people." "You're right, Grandpa. I'm sure

thousands of people have benefited from that drinking water facility," Sam expressed.

"Yes, Sam," his grandfather continued, " We also conducted a vaccination drive with the help of our friends and ensured zero wastage of vaccine. Despite the fact that we had an excess of nearly 250% of people c oming for vaccination, more than the number registered, we were able to obtain vaccines for the remaining 150%. All these actions were managed by me and my friends after working hours, during weekends and without disturbing our work and family."

"That's amazing. You managed your time very well! How about your office Grandpa?" Sam further asked. "That year, I also received various industrial awards such as "Best HR Strategy of the Year," "CHRO of the Year" as I prepared and executed strategies in such a way that supported very well all employees and also the organization," his grandfather said.

"How about my grandmother and father? Were you available for them? "Sam was interested in the family situation. Grandpa replied, "That was the year we spent the most quality time together. We cooked together, exercised together, read, played, watched online movies, and did many other things together. Your dad became the youngest You-tuber, grandma and I became authors together, your dad also stood first in school as I helped him study. I feel I am really fortunate; I got the support of many of my friends, neighbours, social workers, and family, so that I could utilize this lockdown for betterment. I am thankful and would like to show gratitude to nature, our family, parents, Guru, all people in our society for their consistent efforts to make this world a better place to live ." Grandpa & Sam were both emotional, full of a feeling of gratitude and the announcement of the boarding stopped their conversation.

Ruth Grace Samuel

Ruth Grace Samuel is a fashion entrepreneur from Coimbatore. She's a post-graduate and a gold medallist in fashion designing and has big dreams of reaching great heights in the fashion industry. She has single-handedly raised a label "Grace N' Swagg" which has created great vibes among the youngsters. She's vibrant, creative and loves to give a helping hand to others.

Glimmer Of Hope

Scarlet woke up. There it was again that restless feeling, her head was going dizzy and she fought the urge to not puke. It was another nightmare, the one she had been having for days. Her doggo muffin was snoring away peacefully in a corner of the room and somehow that sound brought her a sense of comfort from that silent night. It had been almost two months since the world had gone under a lockdown and her sleep cycle had become the worst.

Scarlet was a fashion designer and an entrepreneur who had just launched her start-up a year back and the thought of it not functioning well was making her anxious. She knew she had to stop letting those worrisome thoughts get to her, but she just couldn't help herself. She then decided to pray because that was the only thing that could truly calm her nerves. After saying a small prayer, she then drifted off to sleep.

The next morning Scarlet woke up to the sound of her mom scolding her asking her to wake up since it was already late. She woke up and dragged herself from the bed to get ready. "Mom! Am all ready, let's go   ," said Scarlet once she had gotten all dressed up. "You need to really learn to sleep soon, or else you are going to spoil your health ," said her mom as she was coming down the stairs. Scarlet sighed. She knew her mom was right but her mind was just spinning with all the possible scenarios of what could go wrong with her business. Scarlet dropped her mom off to the college and drove back home.

Her friend called her up and they spoke for an hour and during that conversation her friend suggested that she start designing and selling masks under her own label. Scarlet wasn't too sure about it since there were already so many masks out there in the market and she really didn't see how it would sell. But instead of sitting and getting frustrated about her business

doing nothing she decided to go ahead and give it a shot. She started collecting ideas and gaining inspiration and slowly each day starte d becoming exciting because there was something to look forward to. She then began sourcing whatever fabric she could get and gave it to her tailors to stitch. She designed a good variety of scarf masks and unisex cotton masks.

Scarlet and her mom were quite excited about this new idea and how it was all going to unfold. The day the masks were ready, Scarlet was having an entire zoo of butterflies in her tummy. They drove fast to the office and the moment they laid eyes on the entire collection of masks they were so overjoyed. On reaching home Scarlet tried out the sample masks and gosh, they were the softest to the feel and so comfortable to wear! The prints were so beautiful and, in her heart, she knew these would definitely sell. She couldn't wait to s tart clicking pictures for the website.

She had to wait until her mom wasdone with her college work and then they would start their mini photoshoot session. Their photoshoot sessions were super fun and hectic as well. During the weekend Scarlet decided toput up a few reels on Instagram regarding the masks, so as to hype up the audience and to gather more views. The next day after the online church service Scarlet and her mom got ready for the photoshoot. Woah! The photoshoot session went on well with their doggo interrupting them in between. After the pictures were taken was the next big job of editing them and putting them on the website and adding all the details and information.

Scarlet knew she had to sacrifice her sleep for the next two days to get th ings up and running, but the thought of losing sleep because of the excitement was something she could definitely handle. So, she stayed up late in night finishing off all the work. Once it was all up on the websiteshe was excited and nervous. She showed her mom and her family before making it go LIVE, everyone was so excited. Once the website

went LIVE, she then announced it on all her social media platforms and was just praying that someone out there would place an order.

The next moment, "DING!", a notification sound on her phone startled her. She recognized the sound- it was an Order! "Maaa!", she screamed, "Someone has placed an order for not one but 10 masks!"

She was on top of the world. It didn't stop with that day, orders kept coming for the next few months every day; people were in love with the masks and their quality and fabric and wanted more. Scarlet got busier than ever in her entire entrepreneurial journey and it never stopped even after the year 2020. The masks went out of stock so many times and she kept designing more. Finally, her business was reaching more crowds and more people and she even got called for interviews. It was something she had never expected that could happen during a lockdown. It was her own little miracle that happen during the lockdown. What seemed like a shutdown moment was instead a moment of rising from the ashes and soaring higher and she believed it was that tiny prayer she made in her darkest moment that God heard and made a way for her. Even till this year in 2021 people still place their orders for masks from her website and her business just keeps growing and she's forever grateful for all the prayer and support throughout.

Dr. Godwin Alex Kiruba

Dr. Godwin Alex Kiruba is a   passionate Oral and Maxillofacial surgeon, specializing in surgical care for children born with facial deformities.He is an avid reader with a special interest in history and fiction.He is also aPotter-head for life, striving to heal the world with what Voldemort didn't have, but Harry had- LOVE!

The Most Expensive Possession

Ahmed woke up in the morning only to find himself struggling to get out of bed. He began to call his parents fervently, but found his voice incomprehensible and body temperature s soaring. His mother heard muffled voices and went inside to check him out. The time they met each other that morning, they were both in tears, one out of pain and the other out of love. Ahmed's father was a daily wage earner, who struggled to make ends meet. Ahmed was a puny child, born to his parents at an old age, after multiple miscarriages. In spite of being warned of numerous health hazards associated with a late gestation, they took the risk to ignite their lives.

The same dawn, Adithyan woke up to a blistering headache and pyrexia. His wife was the sole support he had. The old man was born into an aristocratic family and had the comfort of studying abroad, even when the entire nation was struggling to revamp itself in the early days of partition. Hi s hostility and discrimination were unacceptable and prevented him from making friends.

Despite a million thoughts running in the minds of both the families, the biggest worry was, WHAT IF IT WAS COVID - 19????

Exactly four days earlier, the Prime Minister ha d announced a nationwide lockdown. The affected had rushed to crowded places for panic purchases. Both families lay on opposite sides of the spectrum. Each of them lacked what the other considered as their biggest boon. Adithyan believed in monetary power while Ahmed's family believed in true friendship.

Both families reached out to Karthik, their neighbour-hood chap, who used to run errands, besides working in a pharmacy to fill up his pocket. Being an orphan, he grew up in a rustic way, but began to understand the importance of love only after becoming a protégé of Dr. Avtar Singh. Dr. Singh had lost his loving brother at a tender age due to his family's inability to provide him efficient medical care, which had propelled him to pursue a career in medicine . Caste, Religion, Education, Relationship or Economic statuses were immaterial to Dr. Singh as he weighed everyone on the same scale.

Karthik promised the two families that he would speak to Dr. Singh and try to help them get treated in his hospital. Despite each family having different sets of worries about COVID-19, with regards to age -related concerns and treatment costs, both had to worry about the social stigma and the   high mortality it caused. Karthik requested Dr. Singh to reconsider his decision of closing his hospital. After much contemplation,   Dr. Singh decided to open the hospital despite the logistical limitations and his health implications.

Dr. Singh diligently treated them and once shared with them, the words of an old monk - "Happiness can be found, even in the darkest of times, if one only remembers to turn on the light". By the time their lab results came, both had formed a beautiful bond between themselves in the hospital. They both tested negative for COVID-19, and the positivity of testing negative, cheered up their hearts and accentuated their health statuses. Adithyan turned over a new leaf and ultimately comprehended the importance of love and fellow human beings. He believed that he had been gifted with a new life to transform multiple lives and offered to support the education of Ahmed and a few more kids. Dr. Singh perceived the significance of working harder during   these difficult times and to offer affordable treatment to the unaffordable.

Mother nature has brought the world to a standstill and COVID-19 has provided an absolute opportunity for everyone to metamorphose into altruistic, benevolent humans.

At the time of discharge, Dr. Singh discerned their worries about the expenses and waived off their bills. He waved them a bye and remarked to himself, "WHAT'S MORE EXPENSIVE THAN LOVE?!"

Bhadresh Dani

Bhadresh Dani is a Husband, a Father, a Marathon Runner and Power Electronics Engineer with Management education from Henley Management College, UK and IIM-A and Leadership development education from Scandinavian Institute of Management, Denmark. He has a total of 29 years of experience working with power Electronics products development, Production, Customer support, Sales & Business Development. Presently he is working with Bharat Bijlee Ltd, Mumbai (India) as Vice president (Drives & Automation).

He is passionate about Sales, Digital marketing, new technologies like Industry 4.0, Artificial Intelligence (AI) and Machine Learnings (ML). He strongly believes in creating unique values for his customers and for organizations he

works. His professional career is built on three strong pillars –
VISION, INNOVATION, and CONNECTION.

He is the best-selling author of the book B2B SALES
TRASNFORMATION 2.0 - MASTER THE ART OF
CUSTOMER ACUISITION AND RETENTION. Available
on amazon:

Connect with the author:
Facebook group:
www.facebook.com/groups/b2bsalestransformation2.0

LinkedIn:
www.linkedin.com/in/bhadresh-dani
Email: bhadreshdani69@gmail.com

How Grandpa Became An Author

"Congratulations! Shrima, on comp letion of your graduation ," Malav said to his daughter at her graduation ceremony at University of Texas, Dallas, USA. Shrima is   the daughter of Malav and Shriti , who got married twenty-five years back in Dallas, USA during the Covid 19 pandemic. Shrima graduated in Computer science and wanted to pursue MBA from Harvard University with specialization in sales and marketing. She told her dad "I want to follow   the path of my grandpa who is the bestselling author of many books on sales and marketing. Malav said "Do you want to know story of your grandpa, how he became an author?" Shrima exclaimed, "Yes daddy, I heard a little but want to know the complete story!" Malav started with smile on his face.

"Your Grandpa was an introvert during his childhood, but an avid book reader. He had a habit of buying one self -help book every week from the airport book store during his business travels. He had a collection of   many books covering sales, management, leadership, motivation etc." He added, "When he chose sales as his career, he struggled a lot initially - five sales visits daily, all seven days, was reje cted by customer s and lost many orders. Company pressure to achieve sales targets, many frustrating moments and days, over and above all, work - life balance was a burning issue. But he was man of determination and decided to master the craft . He started le arning sales through books, trainings, from his managers and also from customers who did not buy from him."

 "But how did he become an author?" Shrima asked with lot of curiosity. Malav continued , "He was always wondering, if he could write his own experie nces and share with the world. One day, he saw an advertisement on his Facebook wall about book-writing and self-publishing. He got trained during that one-day workshop. But he could not commence his book writing journey anytime soon, due to paucity of time."

Malav was reflecting "But to his luck, National locked down was announced for twenty-one days due to Covid 19 pandemic and was extended later on. This meant that one needed to stay indoors to protect oneself from Covid 19 virus. O ffice work was to be done from home online, and lot of time was available after office hours and on weekends. He recalled his training on book writing and joined 'Bookathon' for one month. Similar to marathon, in 'Bookathon' many authors start writing the book together, write minimum words daily and post the progress updates on group portal. There was a healthy competition among authors to complete the book on time." Shrima asked, "Did he complete the book in one month?" "No, Shrima, his first draft took around two months' time and the final book launch was after four months. I still remember that special seventh day of Bookathon, when all authors were supposed to announce on social media about this project to family, friends and relatives. Once, you commit on social media, you can't escape from your promise. He announced pre-launch of his first sales book on social media on the midnight of the seventh day. Even we were not aware of it, till we saw his message on Facebook. It was a pleasant surprise for me and your mom."

"We called and congratulated immediately. Next day, he received so many calls from friends and relatives to congratulate him and many books were sold during prelaunch. I can't express his feelings in words . He was on top of the world. In fact , his immediate manager, managing director of his employer agreed to write the foreword for his book "

"Daddy, I am able to feel and visualise the live story of my grandpa at present. I can imagine, book writing is not s uch an easy job. You need a lot of dedication and focus ," Shrima said. "You are right," Malav agreed. "You need to be consistent daily, when you are writing the book. Your Grandpa had many sleepless nights during this journey. Although, everyone was surrounded by Covid negativity, he and your grandma tried to keep themselves away from this negativity by avoiding news and negative phone calls. There were many ups and down during his

journey and he thought of withdrawing this project couple of times, however due to continuous support from our family and his daily meditation, he could save this dream project."

"What was the reason for grandpa to become an author, daddy?" Shrima asked. "There was a larger purpose to write a book on sales. As he struggled to be successfil in sales initially, he wished that young sales people shouldn't face similar struggles in their career. He also wanted to give his knowledge back to   the sales community and industry. Through his book he was on a mission to help many sales professionals and entrepreneurs achieve desired sales targets. Ten percent of the book-sales' proceeds was spent on chari table activities like food and education for needy people." Malav added, "His book was awarded best seller status in two months' time. Some of the corporate companies placed bulk orders to gift this book to their sales team. I am so proud of my dad's achievement!"

"How did the 'Author' tag transform him?" Shrima asked curiously. Malav replied, "His life was changed completely. People's perception about hi m changed dramatically. He was invited as a guest speaker by many social media live show   s, renowned Book clubs, online live events. Personally, he became calm and compose d, as book writing was like meditation for him."

"I am so proud of my grandpa! I have read his book and enjoyed thoroughly. There were many real -life examples of success and failures of sales calls. It will be of benefit to me when I go in to the field after completion of my MBA from Harvard !" Shrima declared.

Shriti said, "Co-incidentally, this is twenty-fifth anniversary year of that book. Let's celebrate it along with your graduation ceremony!"

Mallikarjun Chaturvedi

Mallikarjun Chaturvedi is an actor, model and writer. He is driven to pursue his dreams at any cost. He loves being involved in a variety of activities and hobbies. He strongly believes in God. He loves travelling and story-writing.

Why The Lockdown?

Mike went to meet his college buddy David at David's beachfront house.

"Hey David, how's lockdown going? I'm quite bored, frankly and hence came to meet you."

"I am fine, Mike! I am very happy to see you today! Hope things get better."

"David, I really miss going to college!" Mike exclaimed.

"Same here brother. But hey, look at the ocean, can you notice something?"

"No David, what is it?" Asked Mike, puzzled.

"The ocean Mike, is requesting us not to pollute it. If you ask me, this pandemic is a chance for us, humans, to reflect on and make amends to our brutal behaviour towards Mother nature, and other living beings. Tell me, what gives us the right to kill other living beings?"

"Whoa, man you are suddenly talking like an enlightened soul! Should I remind you that your favourite dish is chicken biryani?" Asked Mike, playfully thumping his friend's shoulder. David sighed deeply before answering.

"Mike, I accept all your allegations. But I have realized that I too, must change my behaviour. Animals are alsdiving beings with emotions, just like us, aren't they? In what way can killing them for our own pleasure be justified?"

Mike fell silent for a while, contemplating, before he said,

"David, what you are saying does make sense. But there is more on my mind, which is troubling me."

"What is it, my friend?"

"David, what do you think is the reason for this lockdown to happen? Diseases come and go; we always recover from the impact. But this Corona has affected everyone to such an extent that a lockdown needed to be imposed. Why did this happen?"

Mike turned towards his friend's troubled face and smiled.
"Dear Mike, in my opinion, lockdown is a chapter written by God for a reason- to send us a message that we are not born to kill anybody. That's why this lockdown happened, to give us time to reflect on our behaviour and make amends. I feel that that basically, there are three types of people in the world. First, there are those who bring harm to other living beings in countless measure - rapists, murderers and animal - slaughterers. The second category comprises common folk like us, who are God -fearing and yet, engage in vices. The third category is the purest among all, who practise love and non-violence- monks. In my opinion, these are the people who truly deserve the earth."
Mike listened to every word, nodding intently. But all his doubts weren't yet cleared.
"There may be truth in what you say, David. But frankly speaking, the very thought of lockdown, being confined indoors, stresses me out. Is there a simpler way to look at this?"
"Hmm, I would also say that this lockdown is an effect of our own Karma- cause and effect. We brought this upon ourselves on account of our own brutality against nature and living beings. This lockdown is just like therapy Mike, to understand who we are and for what purpose God sent us here."
"Okay David, all this is going above my head! You are sounding more like an enlightened soul, every minute!"
David chuckled before saying,
"Mike, none of us were born enlightened not even the Buddha or Vivekananda. Enlightenment simply means meditating on our weaknesses and converting them into strengths."
"David, do you mean to say that we all need to do meditation for our well-being?"
"My dear Mike, meditation does not always mean using Yoga mudras and chanting 'Om'. It can also mean reflecting on your

own thoughts and inner self, meaning, meditating on your thoughts.”

“Hmm okay. So, are you saying that we need to utilize this lockdown period for reflecting on our thoughts and also, trying to overcome our fears and weaknesses?”

David nodded before continuing.

“Mike, listen to me, there are approx imately 48,781 galaxies found till date and in every galax y, there are billions of stars. Earth is also a part of these 48781 galaxies and on our earth each person believes that he or she is the most important creature! Don’t you realize how tiny we actually are, in this whole equation and how little we, as individ   uals, matter, in this enormous universe? So why do we have so much ego, when we really matter so little in the grand scheme of the Universe?”

“Hmm, your points are valid, David. But don’t you think you will be criticised for such thoughts?”

“I am ready for all the criticism. My goal is to make every place a peaceful one because peace and positivity are my two swords in this time . I sometimes hope that this life we are living, inflicting brutalities on our mother earth is only a dream. And I pray that this should be a dream we all wake up from, and realize the value of mother earth.”

“David, whatever this is, a man- made disaster or a natural disaster, I am going to pray to God that everything should be fine soon. Hope our earth start s healing and we again en joy our days as we did, before.”

Niranjan Nikhil Belamkar

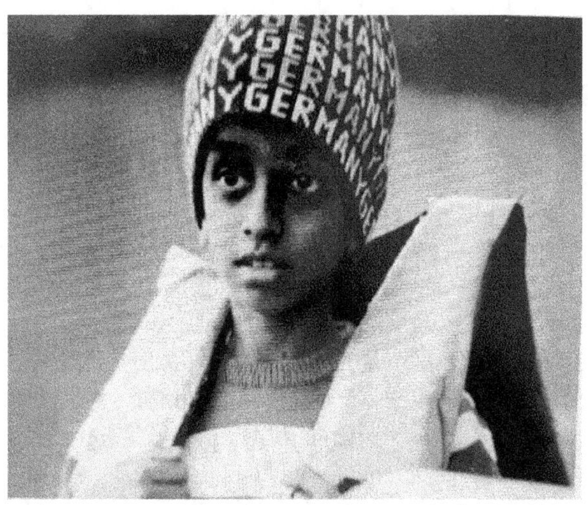

Niranjan is a ten -year-old budding author hailing from Bangalore. He studies in DPS school, Bangalore. He has one younger sibling, his sister Aarohi. His hobbies include craft, trekking, cycling, badminton, chess and of course, playing with his little sister.

Hurray!

Hurray! What a day! Today I received a message from my school that schools will be closed for a few weeks. I told my sister Aarohi and we planned to   enjoy. When I asked my mother why school is closed then she told methat it is because of a viral infection spreading across and that this Virus is not good for kids at all, then I understood and we continued playing.

This is the second week that schools are still closed and we are getting bored. I asked my mother when school will open and she told t o wait for a few more weeks. During this time   , I started observing from my windows and door thatthere are no people on our 3rd main road . I was also watching news for some time and they were showingthat lot of peoplewere dying in our country and as well as in other countries   . They also showed from where this virus came, it's China. They named it Corona virus and I was laughing as I remembered that we had once travelled by a bus called Corona from Bangalore to Pune! They also showed that this virus can be kept away by wearing mask, hand sanitization, social distancing and not going out of our homes. My father never allowed us to go outside of home. This is third week and our school is still closed. But this time, I did not ask my mother about the school's re- opening, as I wanted to enjoy, playi ng with Aarohi at home. Aarohi also started enjoying as her school was also closed. We played board games like snakes and ladders, ludo, chess etc. We both enjoyed winning and losing these games. My father bought me a cricket bat and loved that sticker named Ajinkya Rahane, my favourite batsman. We played cricket as a family game in our backyard.

This is fourth week . My mother got a message from school that schools are starting . Me and Aarohi were not happy but mother told it will   be online classes . I was n ot sure about online classes. Today is Monday . My classes started online through Zoom meeting. I joined and was happy to see my all friends on video! All were shouting on seeing each other after a long time and class teacher was contro lling! Our day-one was only introduction to online classes and the time table.

Now daily routine has started. Me and Aarohi were joining online classes. Initially we got bored of these online classes . But my mother taught us how to concentrate on classes, how to operate Zoom meetings, and then we started liking it . But it was nothing like actually going to school, seeing the school building, meeting friends, enjoying tiffin together and monitoring the class.

I learnt no fire recipe "Veg burger" today. I added all veggies on buns with cheese and spices and guess what it was yummy! I thanked my mother for teaching me. Next day I told my friends and teacher about this no fire recipe and they also liked it. I started liking online classes and enjoying indoor games. But I was still missing outdoor activit ies that I did last year (2019). We had gone for trekking, cycling, swimming and running. I asked my father, when we would go for trekking . He said, "Wait for few more weeks," and I said, "Okay".

Today, my father told us that our government has allowed outdoor activities and we can go out. My father took all of us to Manchanabele dam for a short trek. We took our face masks, hand sanitizers and a few eatables with us. We climbed a small hill and halted on the hill top . The view from the hill top was awesome! After so many months we had come out! I enjoyed this Corona time. I asked my parents when my school would open. They told me to wait for a few more weeks. I am eager to go back to school.

Shreshta Pyaram

Shreshta Pyaram is an autodidact poetess,   exploring herself from within, through her writings.   She ardently believes in 'Forever'. She holds a degree in Psychology. She hails from the bustling city of Mumbai - the city that never sleeps. This coffee addict and foodie loves to travel and pen poems on diverse topics, from time to time. She is currently pursuing her doctorate in Pharmacy.

Out Of Order

In an Indian metropolis, a young wom an is confined to her apartment because of the lockdown imposed due to COVID - 19. She is disabled following a car accident ten years ago and has lost the use of her legs. Since then, she has been living alone in an apartment, because she no longer has con fidence in herself. The grim look s from others as well as mockery, have demotivated her and she lives at home all alone, confined, and depressed. In high school, she lost her feet and also dropped out of school. She completed her schooling and exams by cor respondence. Finally, she managed to get her Bachelorate with honours. Today, Muskan is twenty-five years old and she celebrates her birthday alone like the previous ones. She became a writer and maintains a Facebook page as well as a blog that feeds her d aily. This is enough for her to pay her rent and live a decent life.

Muskan opens her fridge. This is almost empty. It is 9 AM in the morning. She decides to go for some shopping as 6 to 11 AM is the relaxation period. She dresses, wears her mask, and leaves from home. Going towards the elevator, from a distance she observes a red label, unusual, hanging on the doors of the elevator. As she approaches, she can decipher the first words "Elevator is Out of Order, please take the stairs". Using the stairs, which is something simple for others is impossible for her. Surprised, she is troubled and surrenders quickly to the account of what will happen to her in the next few days: a period of confinement without food, in her apartment, which she hopes will be as short as possible. Muskan hesitates at first but then dials the number of the repairman to know when he will come to repair the elevator. She is amazed to learn that he can only repair the elevator after two weeks. She gathers courage and decide s to go ring the bell of one of her neighbours.

"Hi Arhan, did you see, the elevator is out of order. I was wondering if you could do some shopping for me?"

"Hey Muskan. Yes of course. Give me your list. I'll bring everything in no time."

"That's kind of you. Thanks."

She hands her list to Arhan and returns to her flat.

It is now 5PM in the evening. Muskan is bored, so she decides to create an artwork. She t akes out paints from the shelf and dips her hands and elbows in the paint and then sticks them to the canvas. She has a passion for painting, it allows her to relax. She draws the universe of a disabled person in a kind of a comic strip letting her imagination decide the colo urs. She does not hesitate to mix different types of colors. While doing her work, the young woman forgets this lockdown that makes her depressed. Then, she thinks of posting it on her blog and her Facebook page. She takes pictures of her work and posts them on the Internet.

It now 8 PM in the evening, the painting is completed and the young woman is not quite sure how to spend her time. She decides that she cannot be disappointed with her condition and decides to play some sort of sport. She's searching a program for people in wheelchairs on the Internet and find s a program named "Digi-Sport". She discovers that it is a sport for disabled people that allows you to play sports while remaining in your chair. In general, it is a software connected to the Television which consists of a racquet that allows hitting objects on the screen and scoring points. Muskan orders it. Five days later, she receives her package, but the problem is that the elevator is still out of order and that the delivery man cannot carry it alone. She hesitates but as she doesn't have any other option left, she approaches her neighbour to request if he can help the delivery person:

"Hello," said Muskan.

"Hi Muskan," her neighbour replies, "Do you need a favo ur again?"

Muskan explains the situation to him and the neighbo ur tells her that it is okay. He goes downstairs to help the delivery man. Once they have brought the package to her flat, he even helps the delivery boy open and assemble the machine. Muskan thanks them both and a few moments later, she gets addicted to it and plays it daily.

It's been three weeks now since the inception of the lockdown. Muskan is very tired of Digi-Sport as she is constantly playing it for a week. It is time for her to find a new hobby! After several hours of research on the Internet, she finds the fabulous idea of trying cooking as a hobby. The next day, she flips through the cooking magazines that she has always kept without even having a look. She open s a magazine named Kitchen Khazana and on page 93, she comes across a recipe. The dish then gets cooked amazingly well. Muskan then becomes sad and decides to sleep because memories of good moments spent with her grandmother resurface. That recipe she cooked was none other than "Palak Paneer": a dish associated with an amazing memory , that she has never had the joy of eating since the day her grandmother passed away. First feast, first success ! Thanks to her extraordinary cuisine, she can offer it to all the people who have helped her, especially her neighbour Arhan. She is sleepless so she decides to invite Arhan to dinner which he gladly accepts. He goes to her house and before dinner, they play "UNO". After having won four games in a row, by multiplying the +4 and +2 cards, the young woman offers him Palak Paneer, which he eats gladly. Muskan gets along really well with Arhan. It is, she hopes, the start of a great friendship story but little d oes she know that it is actually the start of an amazing love story!

Flairs and Glairs, a platform by a student for   the students. We are esteemed youth struggling to carve out our path for our future and we follow a basic mindset Since everyone is not born with allround skills. Joining hands with people who are born to execute it with perfection is the best way to evol ve. Self-Evolution is the need of the hour but, evolving as a community is what we strive for.   The initiative as kickstarted by, Founder - Mr. Shubham Shah with the motive to utilize the skillset and talent of writing has now a team of 10+ people who are actively participating into newer forms of learning and discovering talents among youngsters. We Provide platform and services like Publishing opportunities, Open mics, Workshops, Hands-on training. Operating with Brand Name of Flairs and Glairs (Publication House), we offer the chance of elevating a passionate writer to an esteemed author   With Brand name Teekhe Zasbaaat. We bring to you an opportunity to get accustomed with the Public Speaking and Presenting of Thoughts along with regular challen ges to brush up your inking spirit.   The newest initiative to extend our services we introduced in a new writing Platform- The Glittering Fables and Ink Over Tears.

We Choose to Fly Like A Falcon than to be

a Leg Pulling Crab.

To Know More: Infoline – 7781900870
Mail Us At-
flairsandglairs@gmail.com / info@flairsandglairs.in
Or Visit is at
www.flairsandglairs.com / www.flairsandglairs.in
Social Handles- @flairsandglairs @teekhezasbaaat